Best Loved Stories

ALICE IN WONDERLAND

by Lewis Carroll

abridged edition

Down the Rabbit Hole

Alice was beginning to get very tired of sitting by her sister with nothing to do.

So she was considering whether making a daisy chain would be worth the trouble of getting up and picking the daisies, when suddenly a White Rabbit with pink eyes ran close by her.

There was nothing so *very* remarkable in that; nor did Alice think it so *very* much out of the way to hear the Rabbit say, "Oh, dear! I shall be too late!" But, when the Rabbit actually *took a watch out of its waistcoat pocket,* and looked at it, Alice started to her feet, for it flashed across her mind that she had never seen a rabbit with either a waistcoat pocket, or a watch to take out of it. She ran across the field after it, and was just in time to see it pop down a large rabbit hole under the hedge.

In another moment down went Alice after it, never once considering how in the world she was to get out again.

The rabbit hole went straight on like a tunnel for some way, and then suddenly she found herself falling down what seemed to be a very deep well.

First, she tried to look down and make out what she was coming to, but it was too dark to see anything. Then she looked at the sides of the well, and noticed that they were filled with cupboards and bookshelves. Here and there she saw maps and pictures hung upon pegs.

"Well!" thought Alice to herself. "After such a fall as this, I shall think nothing of tumbling downstairs! How brave they'll all think me at home!"

Would the fall *never* come to an end? "I wonder how many miles I've fallen by this time?" she said aloud. "I must be getting somewhere near the centre of the earth — that would be four thousand miles down, I think —" (for, you see, Alice had learnt several things of this sort and though this was not a *very* good opportunity for showing off her knowledge, still it was good practice to say it over) "— but then I wonder what Latitude or Longitude I've got to?" (Alice had not the slightest idea what Latitude was, or Longitude, but she thought they were grand words to say.)

Down, down, down. Alice soon began talking again. "Dinah'll miss me very much tonight, I should think!" (Dinah was the cat.) "I hope they'll remember her saucer of milk at teatime. Dinah, my dear! I wish you were down here with me! There are no mice, but you might catch a bat, and that's very like a mouse. Do cats eat bats, I wonder?" And Alice began to get rather sleepy, and went on saying to herself, in a dreamy sort of way, "Do cats eat bats? Do cats eat bats?" and sometimes, "Do bats eat cats?" She felt that she was dozing off and had just begun to dream that she was walking hand in hand with Dinah, when suddenly, thump! thump! down she came upon a heap of sticks and dry leaves, and the fall was over.

Alice was not hurt, and she jumped up on to her feet. It was all dark overhead. Before her was another long passage, and the White Rabbit was still in sight, hurrying down it.

Away went Alice like the wind, and she was just in time to hear it say, "Oh, my ears and whiskers, how late it's getting!" Suddenly the Rabbit was no longer to be seen. She found herself in a long, low hall, lit up by a row of lamps hanging from the roof.

There were doors all around the hall, but they were all locked; and Alice walked sadly down the middle, wondering how she was ever to get out.

Suddenly she came upon a little table. There was a tiny golden key on it. But, alas! the key was too small; it would not open any of of the doors. However, on the second time round, she came upon a low curtain. Behind it was a door about fifteen inches high. She tried the key in the lock and it fitted!

Alice found that it led into a small passage. She knelt down and looked along the passage into the loveliest garden. How she longed to wander among those bright flowers and those cool fountains, but she could not even get her head through the doorway. "Oh, how I wish I could shut up like a telescope! I think I could, if I only knew how to begin." thought Alice. She went back to the table. This time she found a little bottle on it and tied round the neck of the bottle was a label, with the words "DRINK ME" beautifully printed on it in large letters.

It was all very well to say "Drink me", but the wise

little Alice was not going to do *that* in a hurry. "No, I'll look first," she said, "and see whether it's marked '*Poison*' or not."

She had never forgotten that, if you drink much from a bottle marked "Poison", it is certain to disagree with you.

However, this bottle was *not* marked "Poison", so Alice ventured to taste it, and, finding it very nice, she very soon finished it off.

"What a curious feeling!" said Alice. "I must be shutting up like a telescope!"

And so it was — she was now only ten inches high, and her face brightened up at the thought that she was now the right size for going through the little door into the lovely garden. First, however, she waited for a few minutes to see if she was going to shrink any farther.

After a while, finding that nothing more happened, she decided on going into the garden at once. But, alas! She found she had forgotten the little key, and could not possibly reach it. She could see it through the glass, and she tried her best to climb up one of the legs, but it was too slippery, and the poor little thing sat down and cried.

"Come, there's no use in crying like that!" said Alice to herself sharply.

Soon, her eye fell on a little glass box that was lying under the table. She opened it, and found in it a very small cake, on which the words "EAT ME" were beautifully marked in currants. "Well, I'll eat

it," said Alice, "and I don't care what happens!"

So she set to work, and very soon finished off the cake.

The Pool of Tears

"Curiouser and curiouser!" cried Alice. "Now I'm opening out like the largest telescope that ever was! Good-bye feet!" They seemed to be almost out of sight, they were getting so far off. "Oh, I wonder who will put on your shoes and stockings for you now? *I* shall be a great deal too far off — but I must be kind to them," thought Alice, "or perhaps they won't walk the way I want to go! I'll give them a new pair of boots every Christmas. How odd the directions will look!"

Alice's Right Foot Esq.
Hearthrug,
near the Fender,
(with Alice's Love).

Just then her head struck the roof. She was now more than nine feet high, and she at once took up the little golden key and hurried off to the garden door.

Poor Alice! It was as much as she could do, lying down on one side, to look into the garden with one eye. She sat down and began to cry again.

"You ought to be ashamed of yourself," said

Alice, "to go on crying in this way!" But she went on shedding gallons of tears, until there was a large pool round her, four inches deep and reaching half down the hall.

After a time she heard a little pattering of feet in the distance, and she hastily dried her eyes to see what was coming. It was the White Rabbit returning, splendidly dressed, with a pair of white kid gloves in one hand and a large fan in the other. He came trotting in a great hurry, muttering to himself as he came, "Oh! The Duchess, the Duchess! Oh! *Won't* she be savage if I've kept her waiting!"

Alice felt so desperate that she was ready to ask help of anyone — so, when the Rabbit came near her, she began, in a low, timid voice. "If you please, Sir —"

The Rabbit started violently, dropped the white kid gloves and the fan, and scurried away into the darkness as hard as he could go.

Alice took up the fan and gloves, and, as the hall was very hot, she began fanning herself.

After a while, she looked down at her hands, and was surprised to see that she had put on one of the Rabbit's little white kid gloves. "I must be growing small again," she thought. She got up and went to the table to measure herself by it, and found that, as nearly as she could guess, she was now about two feet high, and was shrinking rapidly.

The cause of this was the fan she was holding, and she dropped it hastily, just in time to save herself from shrinking away altogether. "That *was* a narrow escape!" said Alice, very glad to find herself still in existence. "And now for the garden!" And she ran back to the little door. But, alas! it was shut again, and the little golden key was lying on the glass table as before. "And things are worse than ever," thought the poor child, "for I never was so small as this before, never! And I declare it's too bad, that it is!"

As she said these words her foot slipped, and in another moment, splash! she was up to her chin in salt water. Her first idea was that she had somehow fallen into the sea. However, she soon made out that she was in the pool of tears which she had wept when she was nine feet high.

"I wish I hadn't cried so much!" said Alice, as she swam about, trying to find her way out. "I shall be punished for it now, I suppose, by being drowned in my own tears!"

Just then she heard something splashing about in the pool a little way off, and soon made out that it was a mouse that had slipped in like herself.

"Would it be of any use," thought Alice, "to speak to this mouse? Everything is so out-of-the-way down here that I should think very likely it can talk. At any rate, there's no harm in trying." So she began, "O Mouse, do you know the way out of this pool? I am very tired of swimming about here, Mouse!" (Alice thought this must be the right way of speaking to a mouse.)

The mouse looked at her rather inquisitively but it said nothing.

"Perhaps it doesn't understand English," thought Alice. "I daresay it's a French mouse." So she began again, "*Où est ma chatte?*" which was the first sentence in her French lesson book.

The mouse gave a sudden leap out of the water, and seemed to quiver all over with fright.

"Oh, I beg your pardon!" cried Alice hastily. "I forgot you didn't like cats."

"Not like cats!" cried the Mouse in a shrill, passionate voice. "Would *you* like cats, if you were me?"

"Well, perhaps not," said Alice in a soothing tone.

"Don't be angry about it. And yet I wish I could show you our cat Dinah. I think you'd take a fancy to cats, if you could only see her," Alice went on, half to herself, as she swam lazily about in the pool. "She sits purring by the fire, licking her paws and washing her face — and she's such a capital one for catching mice — oh, I beg your pardon!" cried Alice again, for this time the Mouse was bristling all over. "We won't talk about her any more."

"We, indeed!" cried the Mouse, who was trembling down to the end of its tail. "As if I would talk on such a subject! Our family always hated cats — nasty, low, vulgar things! Don't let me hear the name again!"

"I won't indeed!" said Alice, in a hurry to change the subject of conversation. "Are you — are you fond — of — of dogs?"

The Mouse did not answer, so Alice went on eagerly, "There is such a nice little dog, near our house! A little bright-eyed terrier, with oh, such long curly brown hair! And it'll fetch things when you throw them, and all sorts of things — and it belongs to a farmer, you know, and he says it's so useful, it's worth a hundred pounds! He says it kills all the rats and — oh, dear!" cried Alice. For the Mouse was swimming away from her as hard as it could go.

So she called softly after it, "Mouse, dear! Do come back, and we won't talk about cats, or dogs either!"

When the Mouse heard this, it turned round and

swam slowly back. Its face was quite pale and it said, in a low trembling voice, "Let us get to the shore, and then I'll tell you my history, and you'll understand why I hate cats and dogs."

It was time to go, for the pool was getting quite crowded with the birds and animals that had fallen into it. There was a Duck and a Dodo, a Lory and an Eaglet, and several other curious creatures. Alice led the way, and the whole party swam ashore.

A Caucus Race and a Long Tale

It was a queer-looking party that assembled on the bank — the birds with draggled feathers, the animals with their fur clinging close to them, and all dripping wet, cross, and uncomfortable.

The first question was how to get dry again.

The Mouse, who seemed to be a person of some authority, called out, "Sit down and listen to me! *I'll* soon make you dry enough!" They all sat down at once, in a large ring, with the Mouse in the middle.

"Ahem!" said the Mouse with an important air. "This is the driest thing I know. Silence all round, if you please! 'William the Conqueror, whose cause was favoured by the pope, was soon submitted to by the English, who wanted leaders and had been of late much accustomed to usurpation and conquest. Edwin and Morcar, the earls of Mercia and Northumbria —'"

"Ugh!" said the Lory, with a shiver.

"I beg your pardon!" said the Mouse, frowning, but very politely. "Did you speak?"

"Not I!" said the Lory, hastily.

"I thought you did," said the Mouse. "I proceed. 'Edwin and Morcar declared for him; and even Stigand, the Archbishop of Canterbury, found it advisable —'"

"Found *what?*" said the Duck.

"Found *it*," the Mouse replied rather crossly. "Of course you know what 'it' means."

"I know what 'it' means well enough," said the Duck. "It's generally a frog or a worm. The question is, what did the archbishop find?"

The Mouse hurriedly went on, "'— found it advisable to go with Edgar Atheling to meet William and offer him the crown. William's conduct at first was moderate. But the insolence of his Normans —' How are you getting on now, my dear?" it continued, turning to Alice.

"As wet as ever," said Alice in a melancholy tone.

"In that case," said the Dodo solemnly, "I move that the meeting adjourn, for the immediate adoption of more energetic remedies —"

"Speak English!" said the Eaglet. "I don't know the meaning of half those long words, and I don't believe you do either!"

"What I was going to say," said the Dodo in an offended tone, "was that the best thing to get us dry would be a Caucus-race."

"What *is* a Caucus-race?" said Alice.

"Why," said the Dodo, "the best way to explain it is to do it."

First it marked out a race course, in a sort of circle, then all the party were placed along the course, here and there. They began running when they liked, and they left off when they liked, so that it was not easy to know when the race was over. When they had been running half an hour or so, and were dry again, the Dodo suddenly called out, "The race is over!" and they all crowded round it, panting and asking, "But who has won?" This question the Dodo could not answer without a great deal of thought, and it stood for a long time with one finger pressed upon its forehead while the rest waited in silence. At last the

Dodo said, "*Everybody* has won, and *all* must have prizes."

"But who is to give the prizes?" a chorus of voices asked.

"Why, she, of course," said the Dodo, pointing to Alice, and the whole party at once crowded round her, calling out, "Prizes! Prizes!"

Alice had no idea what to do, and in despair she put her hand in her pocket, and pulled out a box of comfits and handed them round as prizes. There was exactly one each.

"She must have a prize herself," said the Mouse.

"Of course," the Dodo replied very gravely. "What else have you got in your pocket?"

"Only a thimble," said Alice.

"Hand it over," said the Dodo.

Then the Dodo solemnly presented the thimble, saying, "We beg your acceptance of this elegant thimble." And they all cheered.

Alice thought the whole thing very absurd, but they all looked so grave that she did not dare to laugh and simply bowed, and took the thimble, looking as solemn as she could. Then they sat down again in a ring, and begged the Mouse to tell them something more.

"You promised to tell me your history, you know," said Alice.

"Mine is a long and sad tale!" said the Mouse, sighing.

"It *is* a long tail, certainly," said Alice, looking

down with wonder at the Mouse's tail, "but why do you call it sad?" And she kept on puzzling about it while the Mouse was speaking.

"You are not attending!" said the Mouse to Alice, severely. "What are you thinking of?"

"I beg your pardon," said Alice very humbly. "You had got to the fifth bend, I think?"

"I had *not*!" cried the Mouse, very angrily.

"A knot!" said Alice, always ready to make herself useful. "Oh, do let me help to undo it!"

"I shall do nothing of the sort," said the Mouse, getting up and walking away. "You insult me by talking such nonsense!"

"Please come back and finish your story!" Alice called after it. But the Mouse shook its head and walked a little quicker.

"What a pity!" sighed the Lory.

"I wish I had our Dinah here!" said Alice aloud, addressing nobody in particular. "*She'd* soon fetch it back!"

"And who is Dinah?" said the Lory.

Alice was always ready to talk about her pet. "Dinah's our cat. And she's such a capital one for catching mice! And oh, I wish you could see her after the birds! Why, she'll eat a little bird as soon as look at it!"

This speech caused a remarkable sensation among the party. Some of the birds hurried off at once, and a Canary called out in a trembling voice to its children, "Come away, my dears! It's high time you were all in bed!" They all moved off, and Alice was left alone.

"I wish I hadn't mentioned Dinah!" she said to herself. "Nobody seems to like her, down here, and I am sure she's the best cat in the world!"

And here poor Alice began to cry again, for she felt very lonely. In a while, she heard a little pattering of footsteps in the distance, and she looked up eagerly, hoping that the Mouse was coming back to finish his story.

The Rabbit Sends in a Little Bill

It was the White Rabbit looking anxiously about as if it had lost something. She heard it muttering to itself, "The Duchess! Oh, my fur and whiskers! She'll get me executed, as sure as ferrets are ferrets! Where *can* I have dropped them, I wonder?"

Alice guessed in a moment that it was looking for the fan and the pair of white kid gloves, and she began hunting about for them, but they were nowhere to be seen.

Very soon the Rabbit noticed Alice and called out to her in an angry tone, "Why, Mary Ann, what *are* you doing out here? Run home this moment and fetch a pair of gloves and a fan! Quick, now!"

And Alice was so much frightened that she ran off at once in the direction it pointed to.

"He took me for his housemaid," she said to herself as she ran. "How surprised he'll be when he finds out who I am! But I'd better take him his fan and gloves — that is, if I can find them." As she said this, she came upon a neat little house, on the door of which was a bright brass plate with the name "W. Rabbit" engraved upon it. She went in without knocking, and hurried upstairs, in great fear lest she should meet the real Mary Ann, and be turned out of the house before she had found the fan and gloves.

"How queer it seems," Alice said to herself, "to be taking messages for a rabbit! I suppose Dinah'll be sending me on messages next."

She found her way into a tidy little room with a table in the window, and on it a fan and two or three pairs of gloves. She took up the fan and a pair of the gloves, when her eyes fell upon a little bottle near the looking-glass. There was no label this time, but nevertheless she uncorked it and put it to her lips.

Before she had drunk half the bottle, she found her head pressing against the ceiling, and had to stoop to save her neck from being broken. She went on growing, and very soon had to kneel down on the floor. In another minute there was not even room for this, and she tried lying down with one elbow against the door and the other arm curled round her head. Still she went on growing, and, as a last resource, she put one arm out of the window, and one foot up the chimney.

Luckily for Alice, the little magic bottle had now had its full effect, and she grew no larger. Still it was very uncomfortable, and, as there seemed to be no

sort of chance of her ever getting out of the room, no wonder she felt unhappy.

After a few minutes she heard a voice outside.

"Mary Ann! Mary Ann!" said the voice. "Fetch me my gloves this moment!" Then came a little pattering of feet on the stairs.

Alice knew it was the Rabbit coming to look for her, and she trembled till she shook the house, quite forgetting that she was now about a thousand times as large as the Rabbit, and had no reason to be afraid of it.

Presently the Rabbit came up to the door, and tried to open it. But as Alice's elbow was pressed hard against it, that attempt proved a failure. Alice heard it say to itself, "Then I'll go round and get in at the window."

"*That* you won't!" thought Alice, and, after waiting till she heard the Rabbit just under the window, she suddenly spread out her hand and made a snatch in the air. She heard a little shriek and a fall, and a crash of broken glass, from which she concluded that it had fallen into a cucumber frame, or something of the sort.

Next came the Rabbit's angry voice — "Pat! Pat! Where are you?"

And then a new voice: "Sure then I'm here! Digging for apples, yer honour!"

"Digging for apples, indeed!" said the Rabbit angrily. "Here! Come and help me out of *this*!" (Sounds of more broken glass.)

"Now tell me, Pat, what's that in the window?"

"Sure, it's an arm, yer honour!" (He said it "arrum".)

"An arm, you goose! Who ever saw one that size? Why, it fills the whole window!"

"Sure, it does, yer honour — but it's an arm for all that."

"Well, it's got no business there, at any rate. Go and take it away!"

There was a long silence after this, and Alice could only hear whispers now and then, and at last she made another snatch in the air. This time there were *two* little shrieks, and more sounds of broken glass. "What a number of cucumber frames there must be!" thought Alice.

She waited for some time without hearing anything more. At last came a rumbling of little cartwheels, and the sound of a good many voices all talking together.

"We must burn the house down!" said the Rabbit's voice.

And Alice called out, "If you do, I'll set Dinah at you!"

There was a dead silence instantly, and Alice thought to herself, "I wonder what they *will* do next! If they had any sense, they'd take the roof off."

After a minute or two they began moving about again, and Alice heard the Rabbit say, "A barrowful will do, to begin with."

"A barrowful of *what*?" thought Alice. But she had

not long to doubt, for the next moment a shower of little pebbles came rattling in at the window, and some of them hit her in the face.

Alice noticed, with some surprise, that the pebbles were all turning into little cakes as they lay on the floor, and a bright idea came into her head. "If I eat one of these cakes," she thought, "it's sure to make *some* change in my size." So she swallowed one of the cakes, and began shrinking directly. As soon as she was small enough, she ran out of the house, and found quite a crowd of little animals and birds waiting outside. They all made a rush at Alice the moment she appeared, but she ran off as hard as she could and soon found herself safe in a thick wood.

"The first thing," said Alice to herself, "is to grow to my right size again; and the second thing is to find my way into that lovely garden."

There was a large mushroom growing near her, about the same height as herself; and, when she had looked under it, and on both sides of it, and behind it, it occurred to her that she might as well look and see what was on the top of it. She stretched herself up on tiptoe, and peeped over the edge of the mushroom, and her eyes immediately met those of a large blue Caterpillar, sitting on the top, with its arms folded, quietly smoking a long hookah, and taking not the smallest notice of her or of anything else.

Advice from a Caterpillar

The Caterpillar and Alice looked at each other for some time in silence. At last the Caterpillar took the hookah out of its mouth, and addressed her in a languid, sleepy voice.

"Who are *you*?" said the Caterpillar.

Alice replied, rather shyly, "I — I hardly know, Sir, just at present."

"What do you mean by that?" said the Caterpillar sternly. "Explain yourself!"

"I can't explain *myself,* I'm afraid, Sir," said Alice, "because I'm not myself, you see."

"I don't see," said the Caterpillar.

"I'm afraid I can't put it more clearly," Alice replied, very politely, "for I can't understand it myself, and being so many different sizes in a day is very confusing."

"It isn't," said the Caterpillar.

"Well, perhaps you haven't found it so yet," said Alice, "but when you have to turn into a chrysalis — and then into a butterfly, you'll feel it a little queer, won't you?"

"Not a bit," said the Caterpillar.

"Well," said Alice," it would feel very queer to *me*."

"You!" said the Caterpillar contemptuously. "Who are *you*?"

Alice drew herself up and said very gravely, "I think you ought to tell me who *you* are, first."

"Why?" said the Caterpillar.

Here was another puzzling question; and, as Alice could not think of any good reason, and the Caterpillar seemed to be in a *very* unpleasant state of mind, she turned and started away.

"Come back!" the Caterpillar called after her. "I've something important to say!"

Alice came back.

"Keep your temper," said the Caterpillar.

"Is that all?" said Alice, swallowing down her anger as well as she could.

"No," said the Caterpillar.

For some minutes it puffed away without speaking; but at last it unfolded its arms, took the hookah out of its mouth again, and said, "So you think you're changed, do you?"

"I'm afraid I am, Sir," said Alice. "I can't remember things as I used — and I don't keep the same size for ten minutes together!"

"Can't remember *what* things?" said the Caterpillar.

"Well, I've tried to say *'How doth the little busy bee'*, but it all comes out different!" Alice replied in a very melancholy voice.

"What size do you want to be?" asked the Caterpillar.

"Oh, I'm not particular as to size," Alice hastily replied. "Only one doesn't like changing so often, you know."

"I *don't* know," said the Caterpillar.

Alice said nothing — she had never been so much contradicted in all her life before, and she felt that she was losing her temper.

"Are you content now?" said the Caterpillar.

"Well, I should like to be a *little* larger, Sir, if you wouldn't mind," said Alice. "Three inches is such a wretched height to be."

"It is a very good height indeed!" said the Caterpillar angrily, rearing itself upright as it spoke. (It was exactly three inches high.)

"But I'm not used to it!" pleaded poor Alice in a piteous tone.

"You'll get used to it in time," said the Caterpillar; and it put the hookah into its mouth, and began smoking again.

Alice waited patiently until it chose to speak again.

In a minute or two the Caterpillar took the hookah out of its mouth, and yawned once or twice, and shook itself. Then it got down off the mushroom, and crawled away into the grass, merely remarking, as it went, "One side will make you grow taller, and the other side will make you grow shorter."

"One side of *what*?" thought Alice to herself.

"Of the mushroom," said the Caterpillar and in a moment it was out of sight.

Alice stretched her arms round the mushroom as far as they would go, and broke off a bit of the edge with each hand.

"And now which is which?" she said to herself, and she set to work very carefully, nibbling first at one and then at the other, and growing sometimes taller, and sometimes shorter, until she succeeded in bringing herself to her usual height.

It was so long since she had been anything near the right size that it felt quite strange at first; but she got used to it in a few minutes, and began talking to herself, as usual: "I've got back to my right size; the next thing is to get into that beautiful garden — how *is* that to be done, I wonder?"

As she said this, she came suddenly upon an open place, with a little house in it about four feet high. "Whoever lives there," thought Alice, "it'll never do to come upon them *this* size — I should frighten them out of their wits!" So she began nibbling at the right-hand bit again, till she had brought herself down to nine inches high.

Pig and Pepper

Suddenly a footman in livery came running out of the wood (he was in livery; otherwise, judging by his face only, she would have called him a fish) and rapped loudly at the door. It was opened by another footman like a frog; and both footmen had powdered hair that curled all over their heads.

The Fish-Footman began by producing from under his arm a great letter, and this he handed over to the other, saying, in a solemn tone, "For the Duchess. An invitation from the Queen to play croquet."

The Frog-Footman repeated, in the same solemn tone, "From the Queen. An invitation for the Duchess to play croquet."

Then they both bowed low, and their curls got entangled together.

Alice laughed so much at this that she had to run back into the wood for fear of their hearing her; and, when she next peeped out, the Fish-Footman was gone, and the other was sitting on the ground near the door, staring stupidly up into the sky.

Alice went timidly up to the door and knocked.

"There's no sort of use in knocking," said the Footman, "for two reasons. First, because I'm on the same side of the door as you are. Secondly, because they're making such a noise inside, no one could possibly hear you."

And certainly there *was* a most extraordinary

noise going on within — a constant howling and sneezing, and every now and then a great crash, as if a dish or kettle had been broken to pieces.

"Please, then," said Alice, "how am I to get in?"

"*Are* you to get in at all?" said the Footman. "That's the first question, you know."

"Oh, there's no use in talking to him," said Alice desperately. "He's perfectly idiotic!" And she opened the door and went in.

The door led right into a large kitchen, which was full of smoke. The Duchess was sitting on a three-legged stool in the middle, nursing a baby. The cook was leaning over the fire, stirring a large cauldron which seemed to be full of soup.

"There's certainly too much pepper in that soup!" Alice said to herself.

There was certainly too much of it in the *air*. Even the Duchess sneezed occasionally; and, as for the baby, it was sneezing and howling alternately without a moment's pause. The only two creatures in the kitchen that did *not* sneeze were the cook and a large cat, which was lying on the hearth and grinning from ear to ear.

"Please would you tell me," said Alice, a little timidly, "why your cat grins like that?"

"It's a Cheshire Cat," said the Duchess, "and that's why."

"I didn't know that Cheshire Cats always grinned," said Alice. "In fact, I didn't know that cats *could* grin."

"They all can," said the Duchess, "and most of 'em do."

"I don't know of any that do," Alice said very politely.

"You don't know much," said the Duchess, "and that's a fact."

Alice did not at all like the tone of this remark. Meanwhile the cook took the cauldron of soup off the fire, and began throwing everything at the Duchess and the baby — a shower of saucepans, plates, and dishes.

"Oh *please* mind what you're doing!" cried Alice, jumping up and down in an agony of terror. "Oh, there goes his *precious* nose!" as an unusually large saucepan few close by it, and very nearly carried it off.

"If everybody minded their own business," the Duchess said in a hoarse growl, "the world would go round a deal faster than it does."

"Which would *not* be an advantage," said Alice, who felt very glad to get an opportunity of showing off a little of her knowledge. "You see the earth takes twenty-four hours to turn round on its axis —"

"Talking of axes," said the Duchess, "chop off her head!"

Alice glanced rather anxiously at the cook, to see if she meant to take the hint. But the cook was busily stirring the soup, and seemed not to be listening, so she went on again, "Twenty-four hours, I *think*; or is it twelve? I —"

"Oh, don't bother me!" said the Duchess. "I never

could abide figures!" and with that she began nursing her child again, singing a sort of lullaby to it as she did so, and giving it a violent shake at the end of every line.

"I must go and get ready to play croquet with the Queen," said the Duchess, and hurried out of the room. The cook threw a frying pan after her as she went, but it just missed her.

Alice went out and was startled by seeing the Cheshire Cat sitting on a bough of a tree a few yards off.

The Cat only grinned when it saw Alice. It looked good-natured, she thought. Still, it had *very* long claws and a great many teeth, and so she felt that it ought to be treated with respect.

"Cheshire Puss," she began, rather timidly, as she did not at all know whether it would like the name. However, it only grinned a little wider. "Would you tell me, please, which way I ought to go from here?"

"That depends on where you want to get to," said the Cat.

"I don't much care where —" said Alice.

"Then it doesn't matter which way you go," said the Cat.

"— just so long as I get *somewhere,*" Alice added as an explanation.

"Oh, you're sure to do that," said the Cat, "if you only walk long enough."

Alice tried another question. "What sort of people live about here?"

"In *that* direction," the Cat said, waving its right paw round, "lives a Hatter — and in *that* direction," waving the other paw, "lives a March Hare. Visit either — they're both mad. We're all mad here. I'm mad. You're mad."

"How do you know I'm mad?" said Alice.

"You must be mad," said the Cat, "or you wouldn't have come here."

"And how do you know that you're mad?"

"To begin with," said the Cat, "a dog's not mad. You grant that?"

"I suppose so," said Alice.

"Well, then," the Cat went on, "you see a dog growls when it's angry and wags its tail when it's pleased. Now *I* growl when I'm pleased and wag my tail when I'm angry. Therefore I'm mad."

"*I* call it purring, not growling," said Alice.

"Call it what you like," said the Cat. "Do you play croquet with the Queen today?"

"I should like it very much," said Alice, "but I haven't been invited yet."

"You'll see me there," said the Cat, and vanished.

Soon Alice came in sight of the house of the March Hare. The chimneys were shaped like ears and the roof was thatched with fur.

A Mad Tea Party

There was a table set out under a tree in front of the house, and the March Hare and the Hatter were having tea at it. A Dormouse was sitting between them, fast asleep, and the other two were using it as a cushion, resting their elbows on it, and talking over its head.

The table was a large one, but the three were all crowded together at one corner of it.

"No room! No room!" they cried out.

"There's *plenty* of room!" said Alice indignantly, and she sat down in a large armchair at one end of the table.

"Have some wine," the March Hare said in an encouraging tone.

Alice looked all round the table, but there was nothing on it but tea. "I don't see any wine," she remarked.

"There isn't any," said the March Hare.

"Then it wasn't very civil of you to offer it," said Alice angrily.

"It wasn't very civil of you to sit down without being invited," said the March Hare.

"I didn't know it was *your* table," said Alice.

"Your hair wants cutting," said the Hatter. He had been looking at Alice for some time with great curiosity, and this was his first speech.

"You should learn not to make personal remarks," Alice said with some severity. "It's very rude."

"What day of the month is it?" the Hatter said. He had taken his watch out of his pocket, and was looking at it uneasily, shaking it every now and then and holding it to his ear. Alice considered a little, and then said, "The fourth."

"Two days wrong!" sighed the Hatter. "I told you butter wouldn't suit the works!" he added, looking angrily at the March Hare.

"It was the *best* butter," the March Hare meekly replied.

"Yes, but some crumbs must have got in as well," the Hatter grumbled.

The March Hare took the watch and looked at it gloomily. Then he dipped it into his cup of tea, and looked at it again.

"What a funny watch!" Alice remarked. "It tells the day of the month, and doesn't tell what o'clock it is!"

"Why should it?" muttered the Hatter. "Does *your* watch tell you what year it is?"

"Of course not," Alice replied very rapidly, "but that's because it stays the same year for such a long time."

"Which is just the case with *mine*," said the Hatter.

Alice sighed wearily. "I think you might do something better with the time," she said, "than wasting it."

"If you knew Time as well as I do," said the Hatter, "you wouldn't talk about wasting *it*. It's *him*."

"I don't know what you mean," said Alice.

"Of course you don't!" the Hatter said, tossing his head contemptuously. "I dare say you never even spoke to Time!"

"Perhaps not," Alice cautiously replied, "but I know I have to beat time when I learn music."

"Ah! That accounts for it," said the Hatter. "He won't stand beating. Now, if you only kept on good terms with him, he'd do almost anything you liked with the clock. For instance, suppose it were nine o'clock in the morning, just time to begin lessons — you'd only have to whisper a hint to Time, and round goes the clock in a twinkling! Half-past one, time for dinner!"

"That would be grand, certainly," said Alice thoughtfully, "but then — I shouldn't be hungry for it, you know."

"Not at first, perhaps," said the Hatter, "but you could keep it to half-past one as long as you liked."

"Is that the way *you* manage?" Alice asked.

The Hatter shook his head mournfully. "Not I!" he replied. "We quarrelled last March — just before *he* went mad, you know —" (pointing with his tea-spoon at the March Hare) "And ever since that, he won't do a thing I ask! It's always six o'clock now."

A bright idea came into Alice's head. "Is that the reason so many tea things are put out here?" she asked.

"Yes, that's it," said the Hatter with a sigh. "It's always tea time, and we've no time to wash the things."

"Then you keep moving round, I suppose?" said Alice.

"Exactly so," said the Hatter, "as the things get used up."

"But what happens when you come to the beginning again?" Alice ventured to ask.

"Suppose we change the subject," the March Hare interrupted, yawning.

This piece of rudeness was more than Alice could bear. She got up in great disgust, and walked off. The Dormouse fell asleep instantly, and neither of the others took the least notice of her going, though she looked back once or twice, half hoping that they would call after her. The last time she saw them, they were trying to put the Dormouse into the teapot.

"At any rate I'll never go *there* again!" said Alice, as she picked her way through the wood.

Just as she said this, she noticed that one of the trees had a door leading right into it. "That's very curious!" she thought. "But everything's curious today. I think I may as well go in at once." And in she went.

Once more she found herself in the long hall, and close to the little glass table. "Now, I'll manage better this time," she said to herself, and began by taking the little golden key and unlocking the door that led into the garden. Then she set to work nibbling at the mushroom (she had kept a piece of it in her pocket) till she was about a foot high. Then she walked down the little passage, and *then* — she found herself at last in the beautiful garden, among the bright flower beds and the cool fountains.

The Queen's Croquet Ground

A large rose tree stood near the entrance of the garden. The roses growing on it were white, but there were three playing-card gardeners at it, busily painting them red. Alice thought this was a very curious thing, and she went nearer to watch them.

"Would you tell me, please," said Alice, a little timidly, "why you are painting those roses?"

Five and Seven said nothing, but looked at Two. Two began, in a low voice, "Why, you see, Miss, this ought to have been a *red* rose tree, and we put a white one in by mistake; and, if the Queen was to find out, we should all have our heads cut off. So you see, Miss, we're doing our best, afore she comes, to —"

At this moment, Five, who had been anxiously looking across the garden, called out, "The Queen! The Queen!" and the three gardeners instantly threw themselves flat upon their faces. There was a sound of many footsteps, and Alice looked round, eager to see the Queen.

When the procession came opposite Alice, they all stopped and looked at her, and the Queen said severely, "Who is this?" She said it to the Knave of Hearts, who only bowed and smiled in reply.

"Idiot!" said the Queen, tossing her head impatiently and, turning to Alice, she went on, "What's your name, child?"

"My name is Alice, so please your Majesty," said Alice very politely.

"And who are *these*?" said the Queen, pointing to the three gardeners who were lying round the rose tree.

"How should *I* know?" said Alice, surprised at her own courage. "It's no business of *mine*."

The Queen turned crimson with fury, and, after glaring at her for a moment like a wild beast, began screaming, "Off with her head! Off with —"

"Nonsense!" said Alice, very loudly and decidedly, and the Queen was silent.

The King laid his hand upon her arm and timidly said, "Consider, my dear — she is only a child!"

The Queen turned angrily away from him, and said to the Knave, "Turn them over!"

The Knave did so, very carefully, with one foot.

"Get up!" said the Queen in a shrill, loud voice, and the three gardeners instantly jumped up, and began bowing to the King, and the Queen, and the royal children, and everybody else.

"Leave off that!" screamed the Queen. "You make me giddy." And then, turning to the rose tree, she went on, "What *have* you been doing here?"

"May it please your Majesty," said Two in a very humble tone, going down on one knee as he spoke, "we were trying to —"

"*I* see!" said the Queen, who had meanwhile been examining the roses. "Off with their heads!"

"You shan't be beheaded!" said Alice, and she put them into a large flower pot.

"Are their heads off?" shouted the Queen.

"Their heads are gone, if it please your Majesty!" the soldiers shouted in reply.

"That's right!" shouted the Queen. "Can you play croquet?" she added. The question was evidently meant for Alice.

"Yes!" shouted Alice.

"Come on, then!" roared the Queen, and Alice joined the procession, wondering very much what was going to happen next.

The Mock Turtle's Story

"You can't think how glad I am to see you again, you dear old thing!" said the Duchess, as she tucked her arm affectionately into Alice's and they walked off together.

Alice was very glad to find her in such a pleasant temper and thought to herself that perhaps it was only the pepper that had made her seem so savage when they met in the kitchen.

"You're thinking about something, my dear," said the Duchess, "and that makes you forget to talk. I can't tell you just now what the moral of that is, but I shall remember it in a bit."

"Perhaps it hasn't one," Alice ventured to remark.

"Tut, tut, child!" said the Duchess. "Everything's got a moral, if only you can find it." And she squeezed herself up closer to Alice's side as she spoke.

Alice did not much like her keeping so close to her — first because the Duchess was *very* ugly; and secondly, because she was exactly the right height to rest her chin on Alice's shoulder, and it was an uncomfortably sharp chin. However, she did not like to be rude, so she bore it as well as she could. "The game's going on rather better now," she said, by way of keeping up the conversation a little.

"'Tis so," said the Duchess, "and the moral of that is — 'Oh, 'tis love, 'tis love, that makes the world go round!'"

"Somebody said," Alice whispered, "that it's done by everybody minding their own business!"

"Ah, well! It means much the same thing," said the Duchess, digging her sharp little chin into Alice's shoulder. "And the moral of *that* is — 'Take care of the sense, and the sounds will take care of themselves'."

"How fond she is of finding morals in things!" Alice thought to herself.

"Thinking again?" the Duchess asked, with another dig of her sharp little chin.

"I've got a right to think," said Alice sharply, for she was beginning to feel a little worried.

"Just about as much right," said the Duchess, "as pigs have to fly; and the m—"

But here, to Alice's great surprise, the Duchess's voice died away, even in the middle of her favourite word "moral", and the arm that was linked into hers began to tremble. Alice looked up, and there stood the Queen in front of them, with her arms folded, frowning like a thunderstorm.

"A fine day, your Majesty!" the Duchess began in a low, weak voice.

"Now, I give you fair warning," shouted the Queen, stamping on the ground as she spoke, "either you or your head must be off, and that in about half no time! Take your choice!"

The Duchess was gone in a moment.

Then the Queen said to Alice, "Have you seen the Mock Turtle yet?"

"No," said Alice. "I don't even know what a Mock Turtle is."

"It's the thing Mock Turtle Soup is made from," said the Queen.

"I never saw one, or heard of one," said Alice.

"Come on, then," said the Queen, "and he shall tell you his history."

They very soon came upon a Gryphon, lying fast asleep in the sun. "Up, lazy thing!" said the Queen. "Take this young lady to see the Mock Turtle, and to hear his history." And she walked off, leaving Alice alone with the Gryphon. Alice did not quite like the look of the creature, but on the whole she thought it would be quite as safe to stay with it as to go after that savage Queen, so she waited.

The Gryphon sat up and rubbed its eyes. Then it watched the Queen till she was out of sight. Then it chuckled. "What fun!" said the Gryphon, half to itself, half to Alice. "It's all her fancy, that — they never executes nobody, you know. Come on!"

"Everybody says 'come on'!" thought Alice as she went slowly after it.

They had not gone far before they saw the Mock Turtle in the distance, sitting sad and lonely on a little ledge of rock and, as they came nearer, Alice could hear him sighing as if his heart would break.

"What is his sorrow?" she asked the Gryphon.

The Gryphon answered, "It's all his fancy, that — he hasn't got no sorrow, you know. Come on!"

So they went up to the Mock Turtle, who looked at them with large eyes full of tears, but said nothing.

"This here young lady," said the Gryphon, "she wants for to know your history, she do."

"I'll tell it her," said the Mock Turtle in a deep, hollow tone. "Sit down, both of you, and don't speak a word till I've finished."

So they sat down, and nobody spoke for some minutes. Alice thought to herself, "I don't see how he can *ever* finish, if he doesn't begin." But she waited patiently.

"Once," said the Mock Turtle at last, with a deep sigh, "I was a real Turtle. When we were little, we went to school in the sea. The master was an old Turtle — we used to call him Tortoise — "

"Why did you call him Tortoise, if he wasn't one?" Alice asked.

"We called him Tortoise because he taught us," said the Mock Turtle angrily.

"You ought to be ashamed of yourself for asking such a simple question," added the Gryphon; and then they both sat silent and looked at poor Alice, who felt ready to sink into the earth.

At last the Mock Turtle went on in these words:

"Yes, we went to school in the sea, though you mayn't believe it —"

"I never said I didn't!" interrupted Alice.

"You did," said the Mock Turtle.

"Hold your tongue!" added the Gryphon, before Alice could speak again.

The Mock Turtle went on, "We had the very best of educations — in fact, we went to school every day —"

"*I've* been to a day school, too," said Alice. "You needn't be so proud as all that."

"With extras?" asked the Mock Turtle, a little anxiously.

"Yes," said Alice. "We learned French and music."

"And washing?" said the Mock Turtle.

"Certainly not!" said Alice indignantly.

"Ah! Then yours wasn't a really good school," said the Mock Turtle in a tone of great relief. "Now, at *ours*, they had, at the end of the bill, 'French, music *and washing — extra*.'"

"You couldn't have wanted it much," said Alice, "living at the bottom of the sea."

"I couldn't afford to learn it," said the Mock Turtle with a sigh. "I only took the regular course."

"What was that?" inquired Alice.

"Reeling and Writhing, to begin with," the Mock Turtle replied, "and then the different branches of Arithmetic — Ambition, Distraction, Uglification, and Derision."

"That's enough about lessons," the Gryphon interrrupted in a very decided tone.

Suddenly a cry of "The trial's beginning!" was heard in the distance.

"Come on!" cried the Gryphon, and taking Alice by the hand, it hurried off.

"What trial is it?" Alice panted as she ran.

But the Gryphon only answered, "Come on!" and ran the faster.

Who Stole the Tarts?

The King and Queen of Hearts were seated on their throne when they arrived, with a great crowd assembled about them — all sorts of little birds and beasts. The Knave was standing before them, in chains, and near the King was the White Rabbit, with a trumpet in one hand, and a scroll of parchment in the other. In the middle of the court was a table, with a large dish of tarts upon it. They looked so good that it made Alice quite hungry to look at them.

Alice had never been in a court of justice before, but she had read about them in books, and she was quite pleased to find that she knew the name of nearly everything there. "That's the judge," she said to herself, "because of his wig."

The judge, by the way, was the King.

"And that's the jury box," thought Alice, "and those twelve creatures are the jurors."

The twelve jurors were all writing very busily on slates. "What are they doing?" Alice whispered to the Gryphon.

"They're putting down their names," the Gryphon whispered in reply, "for fear they should forget them before the end of the trial."

"Stupid things!" Alice began in a loud indignant voice.

But she stopped herself hastily, for the White Rabbit cried out, "Silence in the court!" and the King put on his spectacles and looked anxiously round, to see who was talking.

"Herald, read the accusation!" said the King.

On this the White Rabbit blew three blasts on the trumpet, and then unrolled the parchment scroll, and read:

The Queen of Hearts, she made some tarts,
All on a summer day:
The Knave of Hearts, he stole those tarts
And took them quite away!

"Call the first witness," said the King.

The White Rabbit blew three blasts on the trumpet, and called out, "First witness!"

The first witness was the Hatter. He came in with a teacup in one hand and a piece of bread and butter in the other. "I beg pardon, your Majesty, for bringing these in, but I hadn't quite finished my tea when I was sent for."

"You ought to have finished," said the King. "When did you begin?"

The Hatter looked at the March Hare, who had followed him into the court, arm in arm with the Dormouse. "Fourteenth of March, I *think* it was," he said.

"Give your evidence," said the King, "and don't be nervous, or I'll have you executed on the spot."

The Hatter kept shifting from one foot to the other, looking uneasily at the Queen, and in his confusion he bit a large piece out of his teacup instead of the bread and butter.

Just at this moment Alice felt a very curious sensation, which puzzled her a good deal until she made out what it was: she was beginning to grow larger again, and she thought at first she would get up and leave the court; but on second thoughts she decided to remain where she was as long as there was room for her.

"Give your evidence," the King repeated angrily, "or I'll have you executed, whether you are nervous or not."

"I'm a poor man, your Majesty," the Hatter began, in a trembling voice, "and I hadn't begun my tea — not above a week or so — and what with the bread and butter getting so thin — and the twinkling of the tea —"

"The twinkling of *what?*" said the King.

"It *began* with the tea," the Hatter replied.

"Of course twinkling *begins* with a T!" said the King sharply. "Do you take me for a dunce? Go on!"

"I'm a poor man," the Hatter went on, "and most things twinkled after that — only the March Hare said —"

"I didn't!" the March Hare interrupted in a great hurry.

"You did!" said the Hatter.

"I deny it!" said the March Hare.

"He denies it," said the King. "Leave out that part."

"Well, at any rate, the Dormouse said —" the Hatter went on, looking anxiously round to see if he would deny it too; but the Dormouse denied nothing, being fast asleep.

"After that," continued the Hatter, "I cut some more bread and butter —"

"But what did the Dormouse say?" one of the jury asked.

"That I can't remember," said the Hatter.

"You *must* remember," remarked the King, "or I'll have you executed."

The miserable Hatter dropped his teacup and bread and butter, and went down on one knee. "I'm a poor man, your Majesty," he began.

"You're a *very* poor *speaker,*" said the King.

Here a guinea pig cheered, and was immediately suppressed by the officers of the court.

"If that's all you know about it, you may stand down," continued the King.

"I can't go no lower," said the Hatter. "I'm on the floor, as it is."

"Then you may *sit* down," the King replied.

Here another guinea pig cheered and was suppressed.

"You may go," said the King, and the Hatter hurriedly left the court.

"— and just take his head off outside," the Queen added to one of the officers; but the Hatter was out of sight before the officer could get to the door.

"Call the next witness!" said the King.

Imagine Alice's surprise when the White Rabbit read out, at the top of his shrill little voice, the name, "Alice!"

Alice's Evidence

"Here!" cried Alice, quite forgetting how large she had grown in the last few minutes, and she jumped up in such a hurry that she tipped over the jury box with the edge of her skirt, upsetting all the jurymen onto the heads of the crowd below, and there they lay sprawling about, reminding her very much of a globe of goldfish that she had accidentally upset the week before.

"Oh, I *beg* your pardon!" she exclaimed in a tone of great dismay, and began picking them up again as quickly as she could, for the accident of the goldfish kept running in her head, and she had a vague sort of idea that they must be collected at once and put back into the jury box, or they would die.

"What do you know about this business?" the King said to Alice.

"Nothing," said Alice.

"Nothing *whatever?*" persisted the King.

"Nothing whatever," said Alice.

"That's very important," the King said, turning to the jury.

They were just beginning to write this down on their slates, when the White Rabbit interrupted:

"*Un*important, your Majesty means, of course," he said, in a very respectful tone of voice.

"*Un*important, of course, I meant," the King hastily said.

Some of the jury wrote down "important" and some "unimportant". Alice could see this, as she was near enough to look over their slates.

At this moment the King called out, "Silence!" and read out from his book: "Rule Forty-two. *All persons more than a mile high to leave the court.*"

Everybody looked at Alice.

"*I'm* not a mile high," said Alice.

"You are," said the King.

"Nearly two miles high," added the Queen.

"Well, I shan't go, at any rate," said Alice. "Besides, that's not a regular rule — you invented it just now."

"It's the oldest rule in the book," said the King.

"If it is the oldest, then it ought to be Number One," said Alice.

The King turned pale, and shut his notebook hastily. "Consider your verdict," he said to the jury, in a low and trembling voice.

"There's more evidence to come yet, please your Majesty," said the White Rabbit, jumping up in a great hurry. "This paper has just been picked up."

He unfolded the paper as he spoke, and added, "It isn't a letter, after all — it's a set of verses."

"Are they in the prisoner's handwriting?" asked another of the jurymen.

"No, they're not," said the White Rabbit, "and that's the queerest thing about it." (The jury all looked puzzled.)

"He must have imitated somebody else's hand," said the King. (The jury all brightened up again.)

"Please, your Majesty," said the Knave, "I didn't write it, and they can't prove that I did — there's no name signed at the end."

"If you didn't sign it," said the King, "that only makes the matter worse. You *must* have meant some mischief, or else you'd have signed your name like an honest man."

There was a general clapping of hands at this. It was the first really clever thing the King had said that day.

"That *proves* his guilt, of course," said the Queen, "so off with —"

"It doesn't prove anything of the sort!" said Alice. "Why, you don't even know what they're about!"

"Read them," said the King.

The White Rabbit put on his spectacles. "Where shall I begin, please your Majesty?" he asked.

"Begin at the beginning," the King said, very gravely, "and go on till you come to the end — then stop."

There was dead silence in the court, whilst the White Rabbit read out the verses.

"That's the most important piece of evidence we've heard yet," said the King, rubbing his hands, "so now let the jury —"

"If any one of them can explain it," said Alice, "I'll give him sixpence. *I* don't believe there's an atom of meaning in it."

The jury all wrote down, on their slates, "*She* doesn't believe there's an atom of meaning in it", but none of them attempted to explain the paper.

"Let the jury consider their verdict," the King said, for about the twentieth time that day.

"No, no no!" said the Queen. "Sentence first — verdict afterward."

"Stuff and nonsense!" said Alice loudly. "The idea of having the sentence first!"

"Hold your tongue!" said the Queen, turning purple.

"I won't," said Alice.

"Off with her head!" the Queen shouted at the top of her voice. Nobody moved.

"Who cares for *you?*" said Alice. (She had grown to her full size by this time). "You're nothing but a pack of cards."

At this the whole pack rose up into the air, and came flying down upon her. She gave a little scream, half of fright and half of anger, and tried to beat them off, and found herself lying on the bank, with her head in the lap of her sister, who was gently brushing away some dead leaves that had fluttered down from the trees upon her face.

"Wake up, Alice dear!" said her sister. "Why, what a long sleep you've had!"

"Oh, I've had such a curious dream!" said Alice.